A NOTE TO PARENTS

Reading Aloud with Your Child

Research shows that reading books aloud is the single most valuable support parents can provide in helping children learn to read.

- Be a ham! The more enthusiasm you display, the more your child will enjoy the book.
- Run your finger underneath the words as you read to signal that the print carries the story.
- Leave time for examining the illustrations more closely; encourage your child to find things in the pictures.
- Invite your youngster to join in whenever there's a repeated phrase in the text.
- Link up events in the book with similar events in your child's life.
- If your child asks a question, stop and answer it. The book can be a means to learning more about your child's thoughts.

Listening to Your Child Read Aloud

The support of your attention and praise is absolutely crucial to your child's continuing efforts to learn to read.

- If your child is learning to read and asks for a word, give it immediately so that the meaning of the story is not interrupted. DO NOT ask your child to sound out the word.
- On the other hand, if your child initiates the act of sounding out, don't intervene.
- If your child is reading along and makes what is called a miscue, listen for the sense of the miscue. If the word "road" is substituted for the word "street," for instance, no meaning is lost. Don't stop the reading for a correction.
- If the miscue makes no sense (for example, "horse" for "house"), ask your child to reread the sentence because you're not sure you understand what's just been read.
- Above all else, enjoy your child's growing command of print and make sure you give lots of praise. *You are your child's first teacher—and the most important one. Praise from you is critical for further risk-taking and learning.*

—Priscilla Lynch
Ph.D., New York University
Educational Consultant

*For my WOW group: Cheryl, Herma, Jill,
Judy, Nancy, and Stephanie*
— J.R.

For my pal, Robert McKinley
— D.B.

Text copyright © 1994 by Joanne Rocklin.
Illustrations copyright © 1994 by Denise Brunkus.
All rights reserved. Published by Scholastic Inc.
HELLO READER! and CARTWHEEL BOOKS are registered
trademarks of Scholastic Inc.

Library of Congress Cataloging-in-Publication Data

Rocklin, Joanne.
Three smart pals / by Joanne Rocklin ; illustrated by Denise Brunkus.
p.   cm. — (Hello reader! Level 4)
Summary: Three friends find humorous solutions to several problems
as they spend a sunny afternoon together.
ISBN 0-590-47431-6
[1. Problem solving—Fiction.   2. Friendship—Fiction.
3. Humorous stories.]   I. Brunkus, Denise, ill.   II. Title.
III. Title: 3 smart pals.   IV. Series.
PZ7.R59Th   1994
[E]—dc20   93-34156   CIP   AC

12 11 10 9   6 7 8 9/9

Printed in the U.S.A.   23

First Scholastic printing, April 1994

Three Smart Pals

by Joanne Rocklin
Illustrated by Denise Brunkus

Hello Reader!—Level 4

Cartwheel
·B·O·O·K·S· ®

SCHOLASTIC INC.

New York   Toronto   London   Auckland   Sydney

🐟 Fresh Fish for Sale 🐟

Al, Sal, and Hal were three pals.
They were very smart.

One day they watched Mr. Bing
open his new fish store.
Mr. Bing placed the fish in the window.
He swept the walk. He climbed a ladder
to nail up a sign.

The sign said:

"That sign has a big problem," said Al.
"You can say that again," said Sal.
"That sign has a big problem," said Al.
"It sure does," said Hal.

Mr. Bing almost fell off the ladder.
"What problem?" he asked.
"Is the spelling wrong?"

Sal pulled a big dictionary
from her sack.
She looked through it.
"The spelling is fine," she said.

"But it still has a problem," said Al.
"Please tell me what it is," said Mr. Bing.

Al, Sal, and Hal put their heads
together to think.
"Aha!" shouted Al. "One, two, three, four.
Four words."

"Too many words," said Hal.

"A sign with too many words
is a wordy sign," said Sal.

"You are all so smart!" said Mr. Bing.
"I don't need to paint FOR SALE.
Everybody knows my fish are not free!"

Mr. Bing painted out FOR SALE.
Now the sign had only two words:

Mr. Bing climbed down the ladder.

Al, Sal, and Hal began to laugh.
They rolled on the ground.
Tears streamed down their cheeks.

"That sign!" giggled Sal.
"It is so funny!" shouted Hal.
He laughed some more.

"Funny? Why is it funny?" asked Mr. Bing.

Hal pulled a box of tissues from his sack.
Al, Sal, and Hal wiped their eyes.
They blew their noses, hard.

"Oh, my, what a joke!" said Sal.
"*Fresh* fish? Are fish for sale ever *rotten*?"

"Silly you, Mr. Bing," said Al.

"Silly me," said Mr. Bing.
Mr. Bing climbed up the ladder again.
He painted out FRESH.
Now the sign had only one word left.

Mr. Bing climbed down the ladder again.

Hal shook his fist at him.
"That sign makes me angry!" Hal shouted.

Sal stamped her foot. "Me, too!" she yelled.
"What's wrong, now?" cried Mr. Bing.

Al sniffed the air.
"Of course you are selling fish!" Al said.
"We can see them. We can smell them!"

"You must think we are not smart,"
said Hal.

"I'm sorry," said Mr. Bing.
He climbed up the ladder again.

He painted out the word FISH.
Now the sign said:

"Perfect!" shouted Al, Sal, and Hal.
"Perfect?" asked Mr. Bing.
"Perfect!" said the others.
Mr. Bing climbed down the ladder.

The sun was hot and high in the sky.
"We are going to have a picnic," said Al.
"We have a tasty lunch in our sacks."

"Do you want to come, too, Mr. Bing?" Sal asked.

"No, thank you," said Mr. Bing.
"I have to sell my fish."

"Good-bye!" said Al, Sal, and Hal.

"Have a good day!" said Mr. Bing.
"And thanks for all your help."

Al, Sal, and Hal went off to their picnic.
Mr. Bing stood outside his fish store
under his perfect sign.

Fair Is Fair

Al, Sal, and Hal had a fine picnic
by the lake.
Hal brought broccoli sandwiches
and lettuce sandwiches and pickles
on the side.
Al brought cold lime juice
and hot green tea.
Sal brought green plates
and green forks and green cups.

"Everything was very tasty," said Al.
"You can say that again," said Sal.
"Everything was very tasty," said Al.
"And very green," said Hal.
"Green is a very tasty color for lunch,"
said Sal.

"What's for dessert?" asked Al.

"Green apple pie!" said Hal. "I make the best pie in the whole world." Hal looked proud.

But Sal looked worried. "Oh, dear. I forgot to bring a knife," she said.

"Here's mine," said Al. "Sometimes I use it to whittle a little."

"Cut three equal pieces," said Hal.

"Of course. Fair is fair," said Al. Al cut three equal pieces.

AL   SAL   HAL

"Dig in," said Hal. Al, Sal, and Hal picked up their forks.

"Wait!" shouted Hal. "This is *not* fair.
I baked this green apple pie.
I should have more."

"That makes sense," said Sal.

"Fair is fair," said Al.
So Al and Sal gave Hal
an equal piece of their pie.

AL   **SAL**   **HAL**

Al, Sal, and Hal picked up their forks
again.
"Wait!" said Sal. "This is still not fair.
Hal picked the apples from *my* apple tree.
I should have more, too."

"That makes sense," said Hal.
"Fair is fair," said Al.

So Al and Hal gave Sal
an equal piece of their pie.

Sal and Hal picked up their forks.
Al did not. He looked down
at his plate. "Something is not fair,"
Al said.

"It is very fair," said Hal.
"We would not have pie
if I had not baked it."

"It is very fair," said Sal.
"We would not have pie
without my apples."

Sal and Hal picked up their forks again.

"Wait!" shouted Al.
"You would not have *your* pie
and *my* pie without *my* knife!"

"That makes sense," said Sal and Hal.
"Fair is fair," said Al.
Sal and Hal gave Al
an equal piece of their pie.

AL   **SAL**   **HAL**

"I'm glad that is settled," said Sal.
"Dig in," said Hal.

Al, Sal, and Hal picked up their forks
and ate green apple pie.

 Hal's Race

After lunch Al whittled a little.
Sal read her big dictionary.
Hal fell asleep.

"Grr-ump, grr-izzle, grr-eeee!"
something said.

Hal woke up. "What was that?" he asked.
"What was what?" asked Sal.

"That noise," said Hal. "A scary hairy Thing
with one big eye and seven hairy legs
has come to get us!"

Hal made a fist.
"I will beat it up!" he shouted.

"Silly," said Sal. "The Thing is you.
You were snoring."

"Oh," said Hal.

Now Hal could not sleep.
He took off his pants.
He was wearing his red swimsuit.

"Who wants to race across the lake
and back?" Hal asked.

"I want to read my dictionary,"
said Sal.

"I want to whittle a little," said Al.

"But I want to race," Hal said.
"How can I race alone?"

"I have a smart idea!" said Sal.
She pulled a big clock from her sack.
"Race with the clock," she said.

"Silly," Hal said. "Clocks cannot swim!"

"I will set the clock to ring
in ten minutes," said Sal. "Swim across
and back before it rings."

"I will beat that clock!" shouted Hal.

Sal set the clock to ring
in ten minutes.
Hal jumped into the lake.

One minute went by. Hal swam fast.
Another minute went by. Hal swam faster.
Another and another and another minute
went by. Hal reached the other side.
He started back.

"Yea!" cheered Al and Sal.

Another minute went by. Hal swam fast.
Another minute went by. Hal swam faster.
Another and another and another minute
went by.

"*BRR-ING!*" went the clock.
"Ten minutes are up," said Sal.

But Hal was still swimming.
It took him another minute to finish.

"I did not beat that clock," said Hal.

"You did the best you could," said Al.
"You can say that again," said Hal.
"You did the best you could," said Al.

"I swim faster in my blue suit," said Hal.
"Next time I will wear it."

"Next time I will set the clock
to ring in twelve minutes," said Sal.
"Then you will beat that clock."

"What a smart idea!" said Hal.
"We will come back tomorrow."
Then Al, Hal, and Sal
went back to town.

🐟 A Terrific Show 🐟

Mr. Bing was standing outside his fish store.
The sun was going down.
Along came Al, Sal, and Hal.

"Did you have a good day today?"
asked Mr. Bing.
"Oh, yes," said Hal.
"Terrific," said Al.
"You can say that again," said Sal.
"Terrific," said Al.

"Did *you* have a good day today, Mr. Bing?"
asked Sal.

Mr. Bing looked sad.
"No," he said. "It was a bad day.
Nobody bought my fish.
Soon my fish will not be fresh."

"That is a big problem," said Hal.

"Please think of a smart idea
to help me," said Mr. Bing.

Al, Sal, and Hal put their heads together
to think.

"Aha!" shouted Al. "We have
a smart idea!"

"You need a sign," said Hal.
"A sign will get rid of your fish,"
said Sal.

"That is just what I was thinking,"
said Mr. Bing.

So Al, Sal, and Hal
painted Mr. Bing's sign.

The sign said:

"Perfect!" said Al, Sal, and Hal.
"Perfect?" asked Mr. Bing.
"Perfect," said the others.

Al, Sal, and Hal stood outside the fish store
under the perfect sign.

"Come one, come all!" shouted Al.

"Only fifty cents to get in!"
shouted Sal.
"Everybody gets a door prize!"
shouted Hal.

Many people came to the terrific show.

Al juggled what he had whittled.
Hal danced a jig. Sal sang from A to Z.
Mr. Bing fiddled a little.
Everybody got a door prize. A fresh fish!

Mr. Bing counted his money.
Now he looked happy.
"Thanks for your help," he said.

"One, two, three, four," said Sal.
"Only four fish left."

"Perfect! I will cook dinner
for all of my pals," said Mr. Bing.

"What a smart idea!" said Al.
"You can say that again,"
said Sal and Hal.
And Al did.